First paperback edition 1994

First published 1988 in hardback by A & C Black (Publishers) Ltd
35 Bedford Row, London WC1R 4JH

ISBN 0–7136–4083–9

Copyright © 1994, 1988, A & C Black (Publishers) Ltd

A CIP catalogue record for this book is available from the British Library.

Acknowledgements
The author and publisher would like to thank the staff and pupils at St John's
Church of England Primary School, Fozia and the Mohammed family, Mr Habibur
Rahman, Mr and Mrs Darr of Rolex Books and the staff at The Delhi Sweet
Centre.

Filmset by August Filmsetting, Haydock, St Helens
Printed in Hong Kong by Imago

Eid ul-Fitr

Susheila Stone

Photographs by Prodeepta Das

A & C Black · London

I'm Fozia and this is my big brother, Rehan. We go to St John's School.

Yesterday at school, my friend Betty gave me some sweets. When I got home I ran into my grandmother's room to see if she wanted some.

2

'Nani ammi, Nani ammi, look what I've got, Betty gave me these sweets. Have some.'

'No, thank you,' said Nani ammi. 'You have them. I can't eat. I'm fasting.'

3

I offered the sweets to my mummy, but she didn't want them either. 'Fozia,' she said. 'You know it's Ramadan. When you are older, you'll want to fast for this month, too.'

'Can I start today, when I've finished these sweets?' I asked.

'No,' laughed Nani ammi. 'Fasting means not eating or drinking anything from first thing in the morning until sunset, not even sweets. Wait till you are older.'

'We'll finish our fast at Eid,' she said. 'Then we will eat lots of nice things.'

At school we were busy getting ready for Eid.
There were only a few weeks to go.

Mrs Hudah and Mrs Percy took us to visit the
mosque near our school. We call our mosque a
masjid. It's where we pray to Allah, I've been
there many times.

Before we went inside the mosque, we took off our shoes and covered our heads.

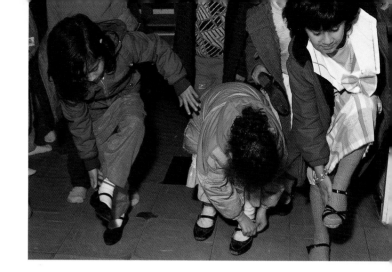

Mrs Hudah, our Urdu teacher, told us about the Ka'bah which is a special building in Mecca. It is shaped like a very big cube. The Ka'bah was first built a long, long time ago by the prophet Ibrahim and his son, so that people could pray to Allah there.

7

We met our Imam. He told us about the Qu'ran. The Qu'ran is our holy book. It's written in Arabic and we learn a few verses at a time. We learn prayers from the Qu'ran, too.

I can read some words in the Qu'ran.

'You are clever to read Arabic,' said Mrs Percy.
'And you can speak Urdu and Punjabi.'
'And English,' I reminded her.

'I know a bit of the Qu'ran,' said Suji.
'And I speak Bengali, and English too.'
Mariam and Suji and I showed everyone how we
read the Qu'ran.

On Thursday we went to the Delhi Sweet Shop.

The man inside the shop showed us how to make jelaybies. Then he gave us one each.

'I like these jelly-babies,' said Alan, licking his
fingers.

'They're not jelly-babies, silly,' I said.
'They're jelaybies.'

On the way back to school, we
stopped at Rolex books. We were
hot and tired, so the lady in the
shop gave us cold drinks. Then she
showed us the books in her shop.

Some of the books had beautiful
pictures. Mrs Percy bought some to
take back to school.

We couldn't help looking at the gold
and silver garlands. People wear
them on special days, like
weddings and big feasts.

When we got back to school, we made decorations for our classroom.

I helped to make a picture of a mosque. Underneath it we wrote 'Eid Mubarak', which means 'Happy Eid'. This is how we write 'Eid Mubarak' in Urdu.

عید مبارک

We made some Eid cards and put them on to a special poster.

On the poster we wrote the five most important things about being a Muslim.

Everyone wears new clothes for Eid, so Ancar and I copied some patterns from clothes to make decorations. We painted them in gold and silver.

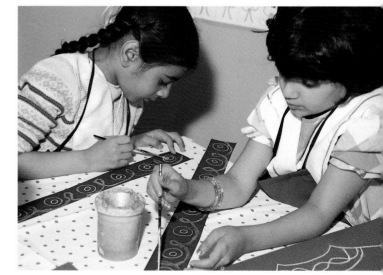

Mummy was making me a lovely red shalwar-kameez for Eid. One night, when she had nearly finished the sewing, she heard a man on the radio. He was saying, 'We have seen the new moon. Tomorrow is Eid.'

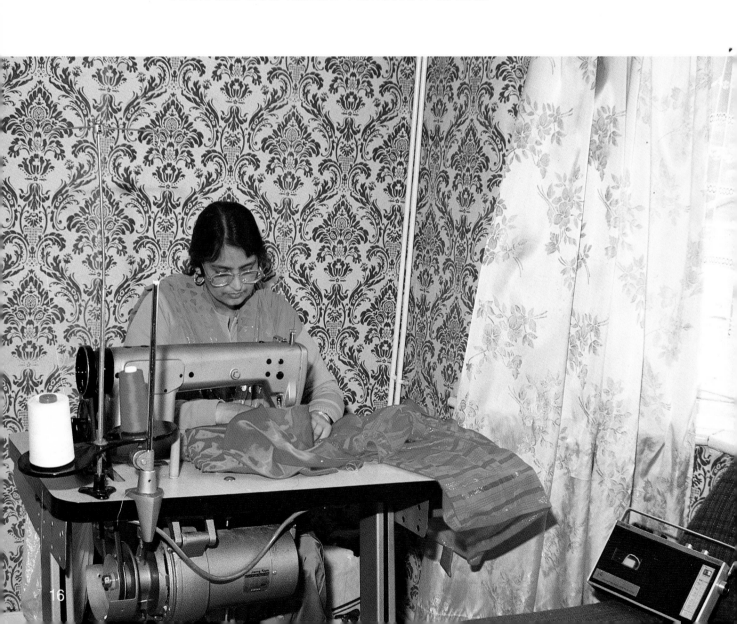

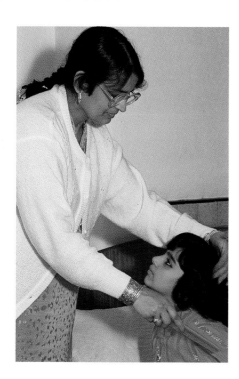

The next day we didn't
have to go to school.
I put on my new
shalwar-kameez and
new shoes. Mummy
combed my hair.

Daddy helped Rehan
with his kurta-pyjama.

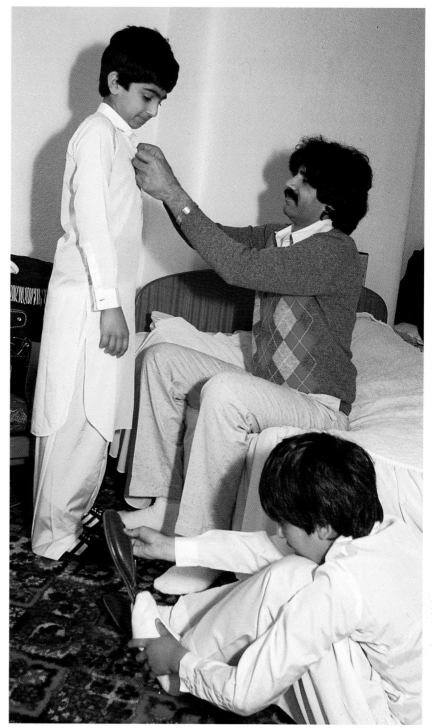

After breakfast, we opened our presents.
I got a pretty toy tea set. And look what I found
inside the tea pot!

Daddy took us to the mosque to pray. There were so many people that we had to wait for a little while before we could go in.

Afterwards we hugged all our relatives and friends in a very special way and said, 'Eid Mubarak.' Everyone was happy even though it was a wet day.

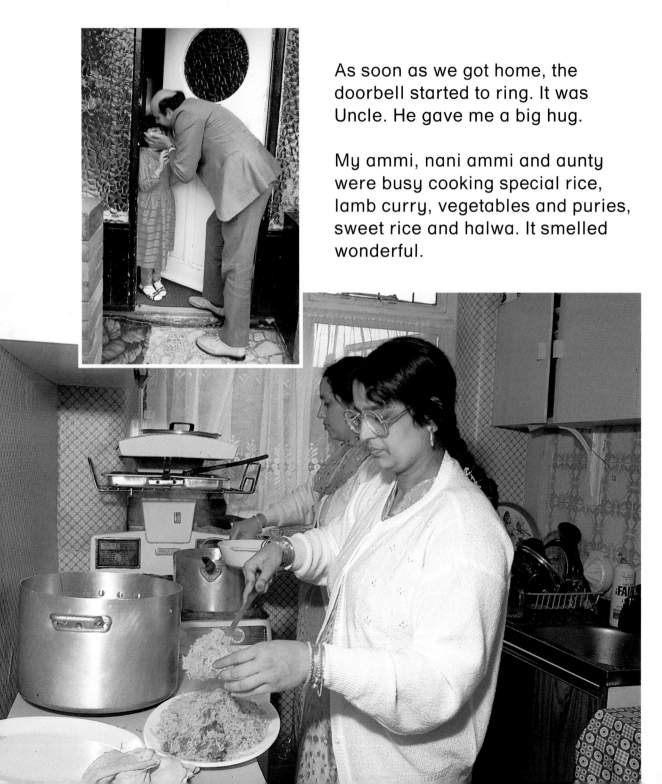

As soon as we got home, the doorbell started to ring. It was Uncle. He gave me a big hug.

My ammi, nani ammi and aunty were busy cooking special rice, lamb curry, vegetables and puries, sweet rice and halwa. It smelled wonderful.

When everyone had arrived,
Rezwan helped to put out
all the food.

Then we sat down to a big feast.

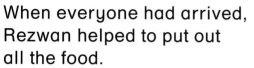

21

The next day, we went to school in our new clothes. All the Muslim children wore their new clothes and our school photographer took pictures of everyone.

We had a party in our classroom and Mummy gave our teacher a box of mitthai.

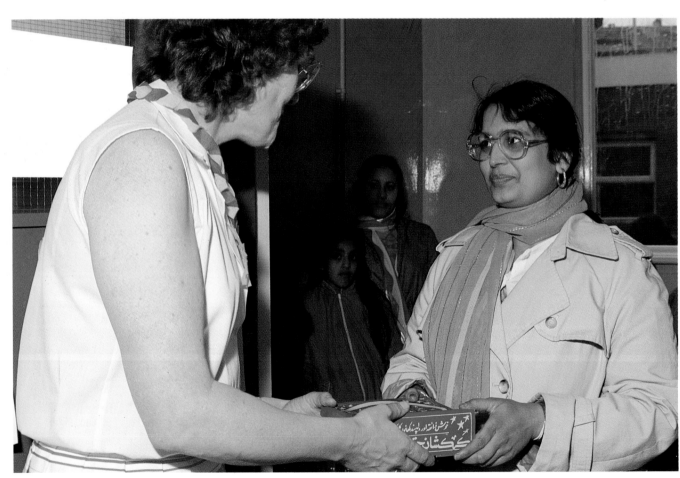

At our Eid assembly, Mrs Hudah told us about Ramadan and Eid. Some of the big boys and girls read what they had written about Eid and they sang songs in Urdu, Hindi, Bengali and English.

I took some sweets home to my nani ammi, and this time she ate a few.

'It's the fasting that is most important, Fozia,' she said. 'When you are older, you must fast during Ramadan. You will enjoy Eid all the more for it.'

I promised I would.

More about Islam

Islam is an Arabic word which means 'submission to the will of God', that is, doing what God wants us to do. A Muslim is a person who 'submits'; he is a follower of Islam.

The prophet Muhammad is very important to Muslims. Their holy book, the Qu'ran, was revealed to Muhammad. Muslims treat the Qu'ran with great respect. It is kept wrapped in a beautiful cloth and no other book may be placed above it. While it is read it is put on a special stand. In the Qu'ran, there are no pictures of Muhammad, or of people or animals. Muslims believe that since all living things were made by God, it is wrong to try and imitate his work.

Mecca, in Saudi Arabia, is the holy city of Islam. Every year, thousands of pilgrims go to visit the Ka'ba in Mecca, and Muslims all over the world turn to face the Ka'ba when they pray. This cube-shaped building is known as 'The House of God', and Muslims believe that the Ka'ba in Mecca was first built at God's command by the prophet Ibrahim and his son Ismail.

Eid ul-Fitr, the festival of breaking the fast, is celebrated each year throughout the Muslim world on the first day of the month of Shawwal. This comes after the month of Ramadan, during which all Muslims except the very young, or old, or ill, fast between dawn and sunset each day.

The day of the festival begins with prayer (salāt) and then come the celebrations. Presents and greetings are exchanged. It is a time for thanking Allah for his blessings and mercy.

Eid ul-Adha, the festival of sacrifice, begins on the tenth day of the month called Dhu I-Hijja and goes on for two more days. It is a festival of thanksgiving. Traditionally, a sheep or goat is sacrificed for each household and divided between the family, friends, and the poor.

Things to do

1. Find out if there is a mosque near you. Try to visit with a Muslim parent or teacher.

2. The Qu'ran, is the Muslim holy book and should always be treated with respect. It is written in Arabic. See if you can copy out a word in Arabic.

Christians, Sikhs, Hindus and Jews all have their own holy books. Do you know what they are called? Try to find out more about them.

3. Fozia can speak Urdu and Punjabi and English. What languages can the children in your class speak? Make a chart to show all the different languages.

4. Make drawings of some of the special clothes which Muslim children wear at Eid. Do you have any other clothes which you wear for special occasions? Draw them too.

5. Fozia calls her grandmother (her mother's mother) 'Nani ammi.' Do you have special names for people in your family? Compare yours with your friends'.

Books to Read

Eid ul-Fitr, *by Kenneth McLeish* (Ginn)
Ramadan and Eid ul-Fitr, *by June Jones* (Blackie)
Going to the Mosque School, *by June Jones* (Blackie)
Praying with Ammi, *by June Jones* (Blackie)
We are Muslims: Assalamu alaikum (The Islamic Foundation, Leicester)
Exploring Religion: Writings, *by Olivia Bennett* (Bell & Hyman)